no quiz

COVINA PUBLIC LIBRARY

3 3774 00182 7881

S0-AAB-619

COVINA PUBLIC LIBRARY

The World of
NARNIA

Aslan

Adapted from
The Chronicles of Narnia
by C. S. Lewis

Illustrated by Deborah Maze

J   Picture Lewis
12.99   3/99

Aslan

HarperCollins*Publishers*

MAR   - 1999

For Mom and Dad, with love
—D.M.

A special thanks to Douglas Gresham and the C. S. Lewis Estate
for their invaluable guidance and advice in helping to create
THE WORLD OF NARNIA™ picture books.

"Narnia," "The World of Narnia," and "The Lion, the Witch and the Wardrobe"
are trademarks of C.S. Lewis (Pte) Limited. "The Chronicles of Narnia" is a
U.S. Registered Trademark of C.S. Lewis (Pte) Limited.

The story of *Aslan* is based on the book *The Lion, the Witch and the
Wardrobe*™ by C.S. Lewis. *The Lion, the Witch and the Wardrobe*™ is one
of seven titles in The Chronicles of Narnia® series written by C.S. Lewis.

Aslan. Copyright © 1998 by HarperCollins Publishers, Inc.
Text adapted from *The Lion, the Witch and the Wardrobe*™, copyright © 1950
by C.S. Lewis (Pte) Limited. Copyright renewed 1978 by C.S. Lewis (Pte)
Limited. Illustrations copyright © 1998 by HarperCollins Publishers, Inc.
All rights reserved. Printed in the United States of America.
http://www.harperchildrens.com

Library of Congress Cataloging-in-Publication Data
Aslan / adapted from The chronicles of Narnia by C. S. Lewis ; illustrated
by Deborah Maze.
        p.   cm.
    Summary: Peter, Susan, Edmund, and Lucy discover the enchanted land of
Narnia where they witness the end of the White Witch's evil spell and meet
Aslan, the Great Lion.
    ISBN 0-06-027636-3
    [1. Fantasy.]   I. Lewis, C. S. (Clive Staples), 1898–1963. Chronicles of
Narnia.   II. Maze, Deborah, ill.
PZ7.A86554   1998   97-2046
[Fic]—DC21   CIP
                                                             AC

Typography by Steve Scott
1 2 3 4 5 6 7 8 9 10
❖
First Edition

Once in the city of London, there were four children whose names were Peter, Susan, Edmund and Lucy. During the Second World War they were sent far into the country to stay at the house of Professor Kirke. The very first morning, Lucy stepped through a magical wardrobe into the mysterious land of Narnia. There she had tea with Mr. Tumnus the Faun, who told Lucy all about the wicked White Witch and the spell she had cast over Narnia to make it always winter and never Christmas. But when Lucy came back through the wardrobe and told the others about her adventures, no one believed her.

Edmund was the next to go through the wardrobe. He met the White Witch, who fed him enchanted Turkish Delight and promised to make him King of Narnia someday—if he brought his brother and sisters to her. Because all Edmund wanted was the chance to eat more Turkish Delight, he agreed. After that, though, it looked as if all adventures in Narnia had come to an end, until . . .

One day the children bundled into the wardrobe to hide from some visitors who were touring the house, and found themselves in Narnia. Peter immediately apologized to Lucy for not believing her before.

Lucy suggested they visit Mr. Tumnus, and to keep warm, they put on the coats that were hanging in the wardrobe.

When they came to Mr. Tumnus's cave, it was dark and cold and empty. Peter noticed a letter, which had been nailed through the carpet, and he took it outside to read aloud. The letter said that Mr. Tumnus had been arrested by the White Witch for harboring spies and talking with Humans, and it was signed by Maugrim, Captain of the Secret Police.

They were wondering what to do next when Lucy said, "Look, there's a robin. It almost looks as if it wanted to say something to us." The Robin at once flew away but only as far as the next tree. The children went a step or two nearer. The Robin flew away again, and by going from tree to tree it slowly led them into the wood.

Suddenly a Beaver looked out from behind a tree. "Are you the Sons of Adam and the Daughters of Eve?" he whispered.

"We're some of them," said Peter.

"S-s-s-sh!" said the Beaver. "The trees are always listening." Then he continued, "Mr. Tumnus said that if anything happened to him I must meet you here and take you on to—" Here the Beaver's whisper became even softer—

"They say Aslan is on the move."

At the name of Aslan each of the children felt something jump inside. Edmund felt mysterious horror. Peter felt brave and adventurous. Susan felt as if delightful music had just floated by her. And Lucy got the feeling you have when you wake up and realize that it is the beginning of summer.

"Now I must bring you where we can have a real talk and dinner," said the Beaver.

So they all hurried along behind Mr. Beaver and presently came to a large frozen river. A dam had been built across it, and on top of the dam was a little house.

Mrs. Beaver was waiting for them, and in no time at all dinner was ready. They had fresh fish from the river, boiled potatoes with as much butter as they wanted, and creamy milk to drink. And for dessert there was a gloriously sticky marmalade roll.

"And now," said Mr. Beaver when they had finished eating, "to business. First of all, Mr. Tumnus has been taken to the Witch's house and probably turned into stone. There's nothing any of us could do on our own, but now that Aslan is on the move—"

"Oh, yes! Tell us about Aslan!" they all cried.

"Aslan? Why, he's the King!" said Mr. Beaver. "He's the Great Lion and the Lord of the whole wood, but not often here, you understand. But word has reached us that he's come back to Narnia, and you are to meet him tomorrow at the Stone Table. He'll settle the White Witch all right. For there's an old saying that says that when Aslan returns and two Sons of Adam and two Daughters of Eve sit in the four thrones at Cair Paravel, then it will be the end not only of the White Witch's reign but of her life."

There was silence after Mr. Beaver's last remark. Then Lucy said, "I say—where's Edmund?"

The three children rushed to the door and looked out. Snow was falling thickly and steadily. Edmund was nowhere in sight.

"There's no point in looking for him," said Mr. Beaver. "He's gone to *her*, to the White Witch. He had the look of one who has eaten her food. We must go to the Stone Table at once, before the Witch can get there. There's not a moment to lose."

Edmund hadn't really enjoyed dinner because he was thinking all the time about Turkish Delight, so while Mr. Beaver was talking, he very quietly slipped outside to go to the White Witch.

After a long cold walk, Edmund arrived at the White Witch's house. There were stone statues everywhere. In the middle of the courtyard was a huge stone giant. Edmund crossed the courtyard quickly and walked through a long gloomy hall. He saw a little stone faun and couldn't help wondering if this might be Lucy's friend. Finally he reached the Witch. She was sitting in a throne and beside her was a great gray wolf. He was Maugrim, Captain of the Secret Police.

"How dare you come without your brother and sisters?" said the Witch in a terrible voice.

"I've brought them quite close, your Majesty," said Edmund. "They're with Mr. and Mrs. Beaver."

A slow cruel smile came over the Witch's face. "Go at once to the Beavers' house and kill whatever you find there," said the Witch to the wolf. "Is this all your news?" she asked Edmund.

"No, your Majesty," said Edmund, and told all he had heard about Aslan and the meeting at the Stone Table.

"What! Aslan?" she cried. She clapped her hands, and instantly a dwarf appeared.

"Make ready our sledge," ordered the Witch, "and use the harness without bells."

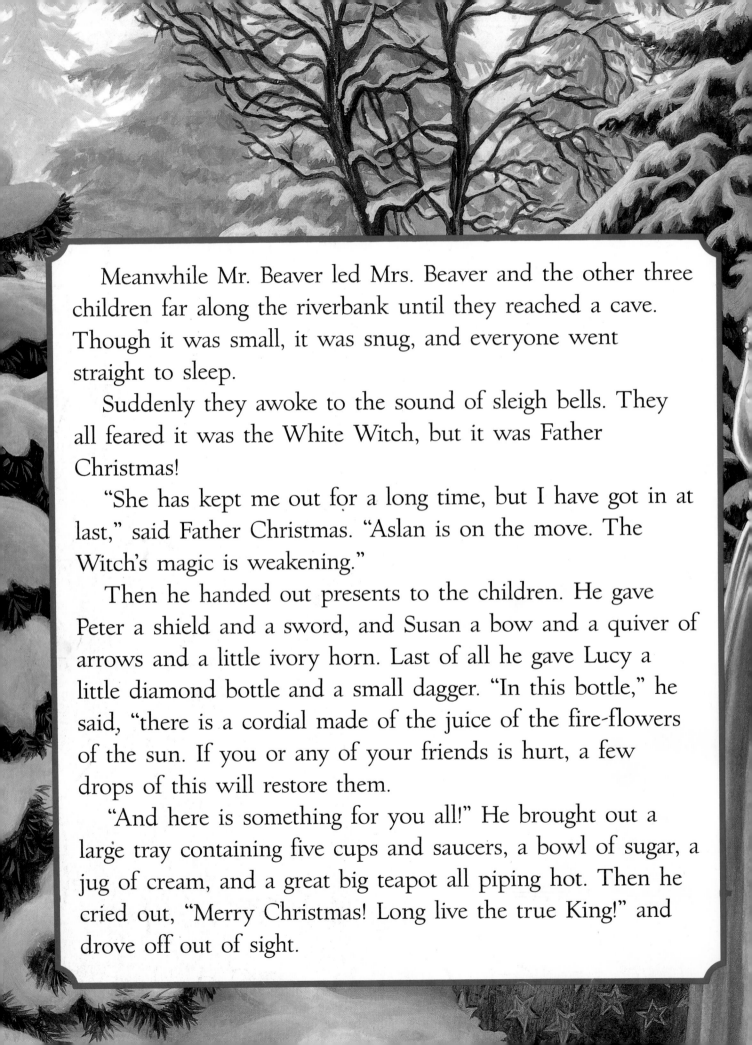

Meanwhile Mr. Beaver led Mrs. Beaver and the other three children far along the riverbank until they reached a cave. Though it was small, it was snug, and everyone went straight to sleep.

Suddenly they awoke to the sound of sleigh bells. They all feared it was the White Witch, but it was Father Christmas!

"She has kept me out for a long time, but I have got in at last," said Father Christmas. "Aslan is on the move. The Witch's magic is weakening."

Then he handed out presents to the children. He gave Peter a shield and a sword, and Susan a bow and a quiver of arrows and a little ivory horn. Last of all he gave Lucy a little diamond bottle and a small dagger. "In this bottle," he said, "there is a cordial made of the juice of the fire-flowers of the sun. If you or any of your friends is hurt, a few drops of this will restore them.

"And here is something for you all!" He brought out a large tray containing five cups and saucers, a bowl of sugar, a jug of cream, and a great big teapot all piping hot. Then he cried out, "Merry Christmas! Long live the true King!" and drove off out of sight.

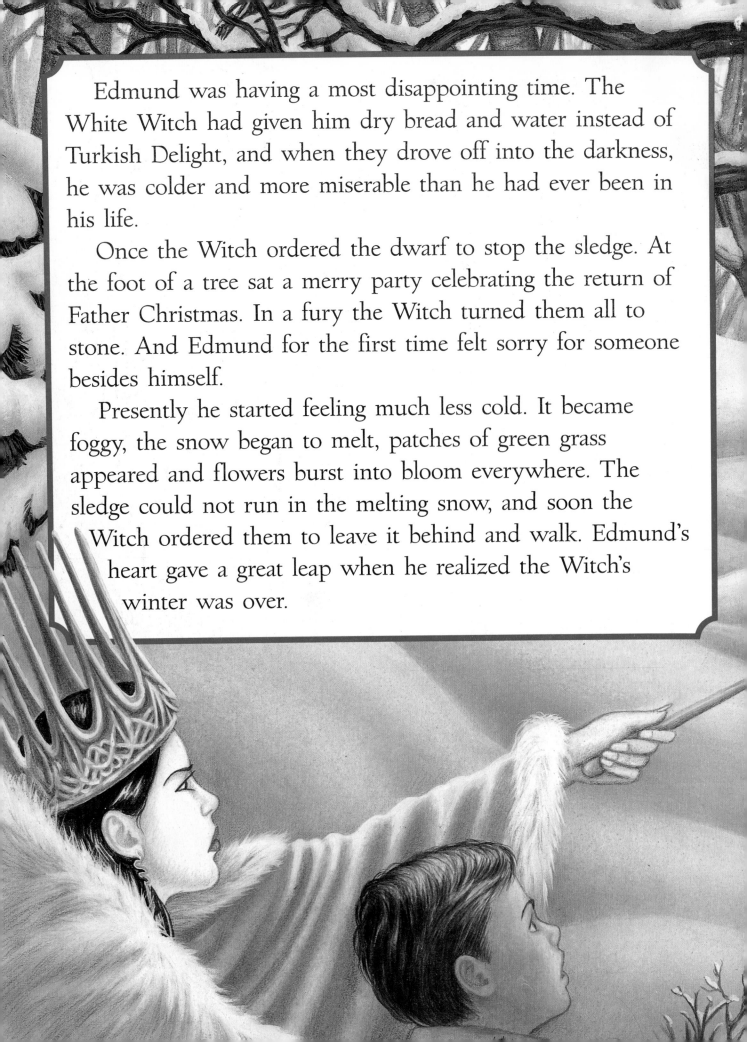

Edmund was having a most disappointing time. The White Witch had given him dry bread and water instead of Turkish Delight, and when they drove off into the darkness, he was colder and more miserable than he had ever been in his life.

Once the Witch ordered the dwarf to stop the sledge. At the foot of a tree sat a merry party celebrating the return of Father Christmas. In a fury the Witch turned them all to stone. And Edmund for the first time felt sorry for someone besides himself.

Presently he started feeling much less cold. It became foggy, the snow began to melt, patches of green grass appeared and flowers burst into bloom everywhere. The sledge could not run in the melting snow, and soon the Witch ordered them to leave it behind and walk. Edmund's heart gave a great leap when he realized the Witch's winter was over.

Meanwhile the other children and the Beavers were walking on and on through cool, green thickets and wide mossy glades.

"Not long now," Mr. Beaver said, and began leading the way up a steep hill. In the very middle of the hilltop was the Stone Table.

Aslan stood in the center of a crowd of wonderful creatures. But when they saw him, the Beavers and the children didn't know what to do or say. For when they tried to look at Aslan's face and glimpsed his great, royal, solemn eyes, they found they couldn't look at him and went all trembly.

Finally Peter raised his sword in salute and said, "We have come—Aslan."

"Welcome, Peter, Son of Adam," said Aslan. "Welcome, Susan and Lucy, Daughters of Eve. Welcome He-Beaver and She-Beaver." His voice was deep and rich. "But where is the fourth?"

"He has tried to betray them and joined the White Witch, O Aslan," said Mr. Beaver.

"Please—Aslan," said Lucy, "can anything be done to save Edmund?"

"All shall be done," said Aslan, looking sad for a moment. "But it may be harder than you think."

Then Aslan said to Peter, "Come, Son of Adam, and I will show you where you are to be King."

And Peter went with the Lion to the eastern edge of the hilltop. The sun was setting behind them, and the whole country below them lay in the evening light. And just where the land of Narnia met the sea, Peter could see a castle shining like a great star in the light of the setting sun.

"That," said Aslan, "is Cair Paravel of the four thrones, in which you and your brother and sisters must sit. I show it to you because you are the firstborn and you will be High King over all the rest."

Suddenly Peter heard a strange noise.

"It is your sister's horn," said Aslan.

Peter set off running as hard as he could. He saw Susan swing herself into a tree, followed by a huge gray wolf who was snapping at her heels.

Peter did not feel very brave, but he rushed straight up to the monster and aimed a slash of his sword at its side. A moment later he found that the wolf lay dead.

"Quick! Quick!" shouted Aslan. "I see another wolf in the thickets. After him, all of you. Now is your chance to find the Witch and rescue the fourth child of Adam." And instantly a dozen of the swiftest creatures disappeared into the gathering darkness.

After Edmund had been made to walk far further than he had ever thought possible, the Witch at last halted in a dark valley. A snarling wolf rushed up to them. "They are at the Stone Table, with Aslan. They have killed my captain. Fly! Fly!"

"No," said the Witch. "Call the giants and the werewolves and the ghouls and the hags to meet me here. We will fight."

The wolf bounded away. While the dwarf tied Edmund to a tree, the Witch said, "Four thrones in Cair Paravel. But what if only three were filled? That would not fulfill the prophecy." After that Edmund heard a strange noise—whizz—whizz—whizz. It was the sound of a knife being sharpened.

At that very moment Edmund heard loud shouts from every direction, and then he found he was being untied and he heard big, kind voices telling him he would be all right in a minute. Then he heard voices saying, "Who's got the Witch?" "I thought you had her." "I was after the dwarf—do you mean to say she's escaped?" But just at this point Edmund fainted.

Presently the rescue party all set off for the Stone Table, carrying Edmund with them. When the other children woke up next morning, the first thing they heard was that their brother had been rescued and was at that moment with Aslan. Soon they saw Aslan and Edmund walking together in the dewy grass. It was a conversation which Edmund never forgot. As the others drew nearer, Aslan turned to meet them, bringing Edmund with him.

"Here is your brother," Aslan said, "and—there is no need to talk to him about what is past."

Edmund shook hands with each of the others and said to each of them in turn, "I'm sorry," and everyone said, "That's all right."

And so Edmund was rescued from the White Witch. But the children would have many more adventures in Narnia before she was utterly defeated.

The Great
Waterfall

The
Lamppost

THE LANTERN WASTE

Mr.
Tumnus's
Cave

The
White Witch's
House

ETTINSMOOR

RIVER

SHRIBBLE

Beavers
Dam

THE

GREAT

RIVER

The
Stone Table

RUSH

RIVER

Dancing
Lawn

Cair
Paravel

Glasswater

A MAP OF NARNIA